Bears for Bedtime!

Storybook Collection

A catalogue record for this book is available from the British Library

Published by Ladybird Books Ltd
27 Wrights Lane London W8 5TZ
A Penguin Company

© LADYBIRD BOOKS LTD MCMXCIX

Stories in this book were previously published by Ladybird Books Ltd
in the *Picture Ladybird* series.

Telephone Ted, Top Shelf Ted and Are We Nearly There? text © Joan Stimson
Don't Worry William text © Christine Morton illustrations © Nigel McMullen
Bears Can't Fly text and illustrations © Val Biro

LADYBIRD and the device of a Ladybird are trademarks of Ladybird Books Ltd

Bears for Bedtime!

Storybook Collection

Ladybird

contents

Top Shelf Ted

by Joan Stimson

illustrated by Kate Simpson

Are We Nearly There?

by Joan Stimson

illustrated by Cliff Wright

Don't Worry William

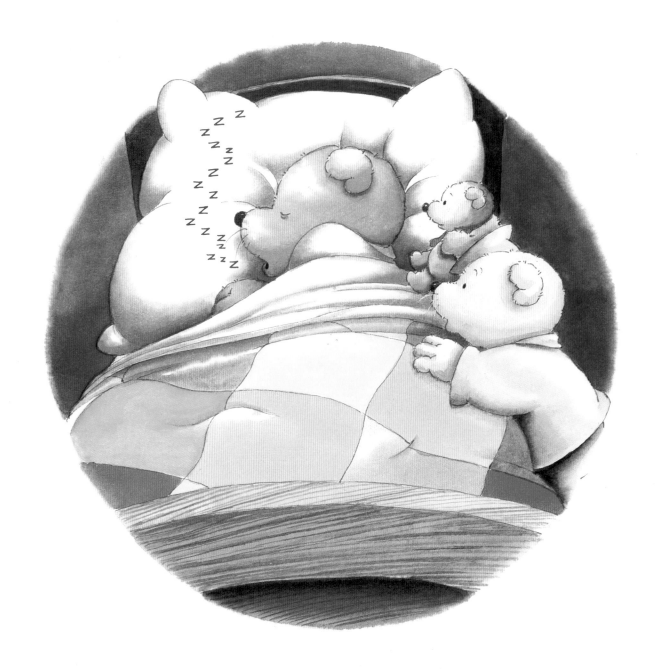

One night, Horace and his teddy bear, William, woke up and decided to be naughty. They waited till Mum was snoring – *zzzzzzzz*. Then they got out of bed. Horace jumped into his monster slippers and the two bears crept downstairs.

Downstairs, it was dark. Sleepy dark. Creepy dark. In the living room, they heard a noise. A whispery noise. A crispery noise. Horace was scared. "Maybe it's a spook!"

"*Tick-tock, tick-tock,*" said the noise.

"Don't worry, William," said Horace. "It's only the clock!"

Behind the curtain, Horace heard a growl.
A small growl. A yowl-growl. Horace was scared.
"Maybe it's a lion!" he thought.

"Mee-ow!" said the noise.

"Don't worry, William," said Horace.
"It's only the cat."

In the kitchen, Horace heard a pop. A soft pop. A bubbly pop. Horace was scared. "Maybe it's a giant frog, gulping in the dark!" he thought.

"Bob, bob, bob," said the noise.

"Don't worry, William," said Horace. "It's only Bob the goldfish, swimming round and round his tank."

Horace and William decided it wasn't so much fun being naughty. They felt a bit wobbly and worried. So they went to find some biscuits, to make them brave.

Horace had *just* got his hands into the biscuit tin when he heard a bang. A Very Loud bang! An On-The-Stairs bang. *BANG, BANG, BANG!*

"There's a th-th-thing!" said Horace. "And it's coming downst-st-stairs!"

They hid behind the settee.
The door opened… *cree-eeak!*
And there stood…
      …*The Thing!*

The Thing was big. The Thing was cross.
The Thing looked a bit like Mum!
The Thing took a deep breath and said…

"You naughty little boy! Put those biscuits down
and GET UP THOSE STAIRS AT ONCE!"

"Oh Mum," wailed Horace.
"We thought you were a Thing."

Mum put them back to bed.
Back to their big blue bed. Back to their cosy,
dozy cabin bed with no spooky noises.
"Sorry Mum," said Horace.

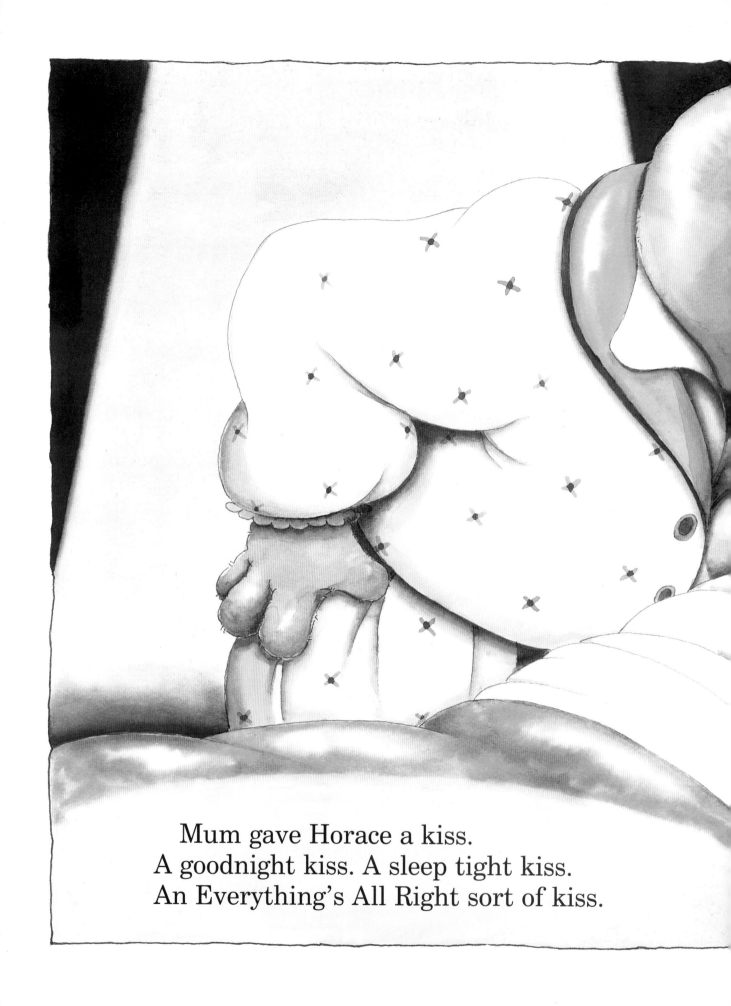

Mum gave Horace a kiss.
A goodnight kiss. A sleep tight kiss.
An Everything's All Right sort of kiss.

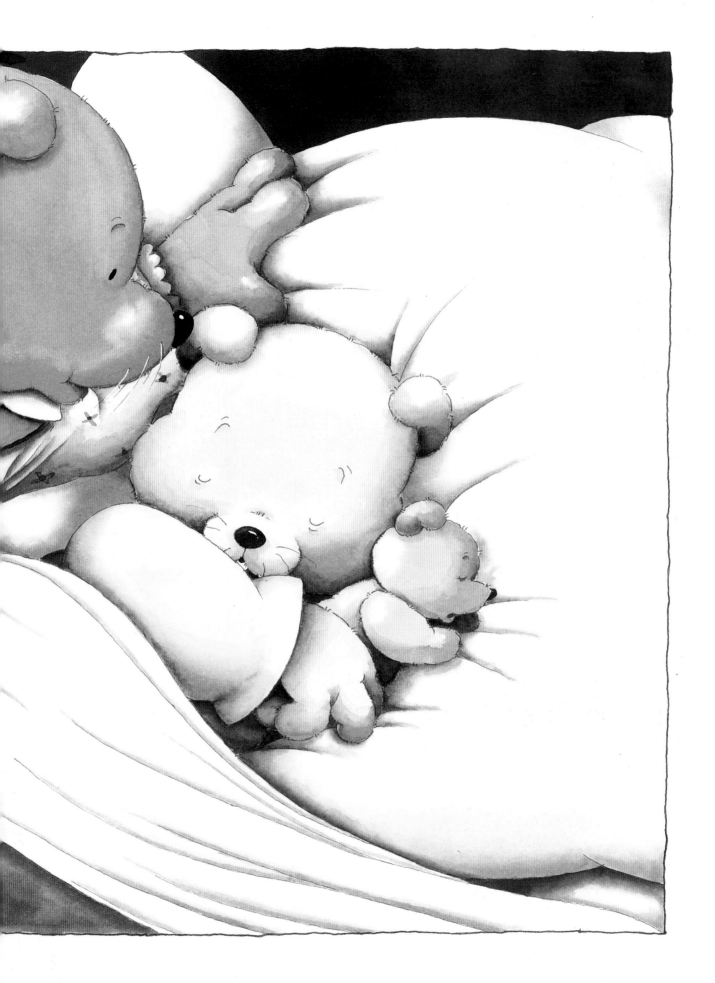

Downstairs, the clock went *tick-tock, tick-tock*. The cat went *mee-ow, mee-ow*. The fish went *bob, bob, bob*.

Upstairs, Horace went *zzzzzzz*. Mum went *zzzzzzz*. Even William went *zzzzzzz*.

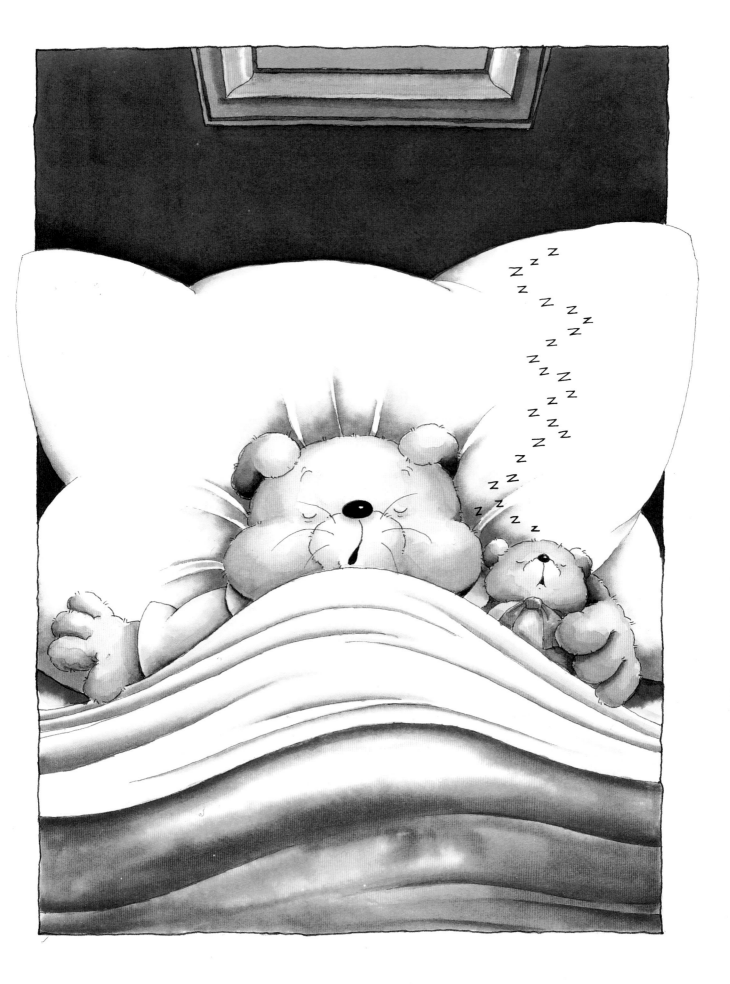

And in the kitchen, a little brown mouse
crept behind the door – and stole the biscuits.

Bears Can't Fly

Little Brown Bear lay on his back after breakfast one day and looked up into the forest trees. He saw the birds flying overhead and heard their wonderful songs.

"Now wouldn't it be lovely," he thought, "to fly about and sing all day. Being a brown bear is boring — all I can do is stay on the ground and growl. I'd like to be a bird."

So he hurried through the forest to tell the birds. On his way he swam across a stream and almost stopped to catch a fish for lunch.

But right then he had more important things to do. When he reached the bank, Little Brown Bear shook himself dry. Soon he came to where the birds lived.

"Can you tell me how to be a bird?"
he asked them.

The birds thought this was so funny that they
laughed until they nearly fell out of the tree.

"You can't be a bird," said Owl, "because bears
can't fly. Anyway, you don't have any *wings*."

Little Brown Bear was sad when he heard that, but then he had an idea. He set off for the edge of the forest where the odd-job man lived and explained to him that he needed some wings so he could be a bird.

"Well, I never!" exclaimed the odd-job man.
But he didn't laugh because he was kind.

Instead, he set about making some wings out of paper, like two kites, and stuck them on Little Brown Bear's back with sticky tape.

When Little Brown Bear came to the stream again,
he did not swim across in case his wings came off.
Instead, he fetched a tree trunk in his strong paws
and made a bridge.

So he walked across the stream without getting
wet and continued on to the birds.

"I'm a bird now," he said proudly.
"Look, I've got wings!"

The birds started to laugh louder still, but Owl
stopped them with a look.

"You can't be a bird," he said, "because bears
can't fly. Anyway, you don't have any *feathers*!"

Little Brown Bear was very sad to hear that, but he had another idea. He went to the other edge of the forest where the tailor lived.

"I need some feathers, please," Little Brown Bear told him, "so I can be a bird."

"Fancy that!" said the tailor, but he didn't laugh at Little Brown Bear either.

Instead, he made a coat out of some spare hat feathers and buttoned Little Brown Bear into it. It was only when Little Brown Bear had left that the tailor burst out laughing, and he laughed so much that he had to lie down.

"I'm a bird now!" cried Little Brown Bear to the birds. "Look! I've got feathers!"

Owl shook his head. "You haven't got a *beak*!" he hooted.

"Where's your beak? Where's your beak?" screeched some naughty crows.

"Oh, bother!" said Little Brown Bear to himself. "Where can I get a beak?" Being a bird was very hard work.

Then Little Brown Bear
had another idea.

"I'll *make* a beak for myself!"
he announced, and dashed
off until he came to a tall
tree. He quickly climbed to
the top and broke off a
piece of hollow branch. With
his sharp teeth and long
tongue he soon turned it into
the shape of a beak – and
stuck the beak on his nose.

There was a puddle on the
ground nearby and when he
saw his reflection in the water
Little Brown Bear thought
that he really looked like
a bird now.

He was in a hurry to show the birds, so he got down on all fours and ran as fast as he could, kite-wings, feather-coat, wooden beak and all.

"Book! Book!" he shouted as he came near. "I'be god a beak! I'b a bird ad last!" He couldn't talk very well with the beak on his nose.

Owl had trouble keeping a straight face.
"Aah, hem. That may be," he said, trying not to
laugh. "But tell me this. CAN YOU FLY?"

Little Brown Bear was indignant. "Fly? Ob course I cad fly. Book!"

First, he lifted his front paws and hopped about.

But that wasn't flying.

Then he stood upside down and kicked his legs in the air.

"That's not flying, either!" hooted Owl.

"Bery bell, den," said Little Brown Bear, "book at dis!"

He climbed to the top of a nearby rock, spread his arms, took a deep breath, shut his eyes and before Owl could stop him… jumped.

Poor Little Brown Bear fell with a THUMP in a pile of leaves and rolled over and over to the great alarm of Owl and the other birds who were watching.

When he got to his feet, Little Brown Bear's beak fell off and he looked a mess. Some of the baby birds couldn't help giggling.

"I told you before," said Owl sternly, "and I'm telling you again, *bears can't fly*. You are a *bear* and bears aren't *meant* to be birds!"

"Wait! Wait!" shouted Bear, determined not to give up. "You haven't heard me *sing* yet!"

And he began to sing in what he thought was the voice of a nightingale.

To tell the truth, it sounded just like the voice of a bear.

A *large, fierce* bear.

GROWL,
GROUUWLL,
GROUUUWLLL.

The birds all panicked and flew away as fast as they could. Even Owl took off in a hurry, scattering feathers as he went.

Just then Little Black Bear came toddling by.

"Good afternoon," he said. "What are you growling about here all by yourself?"

When Little Brown Bear told him how he had wanted to be a bird, Little Black Bear smiled. "I know the feeling," he said. "I wanted to be a fish at one time. But I soon realised that being a bear was better. Anyway," he added, "bears can't fly!"

Little Brown Bear sat down to think about this.
After all, many birds can't swim or catch fish.
They can't carry tree trunks or build bridges,
and they certainly had no teeth or long tongues.
What's more, they can't run on two legs nearly as
fast as he can on all fours.

"Perhaps being a bear is not so bad after all," he
said to his new friend.

"Best of all," said Little Black Bear, "birds don't live in warm, snug dens like we bears do. Tell you what, why don't you come back to my den? There's honey for tea."

"Oh, yes please!" cried Little Brown Bear and jumped to his feet. He took off his tattered feather-coat and threw away his ridiculous wings.

"Flying and singing are all very well, but being a bear – " he said, thinking about the honey, "is much, much, MUCH better!"

Telephone
-TED-

The Teddy at Number Ten was bored.
His owner had just started school.
And Ted had too much time on his paws.

Brring, brring. Ted waited for Charlie's
mum to answer the phone. But the
washing machine was going flat out.
And she couldn't hear it.

Brring, brring...
Ted peeked round
the door.

Brring, brring...
he clambered
onto a chair.

And then...
brring, brring...
Ted picked up
the receiver!

"It's only me," said a cheerful voice. "I'd like to pop round after school and bring a cake."

Ted listened eagerly. Then he took a deep breath:

"Hi there, Grandma, that sounds great,
But what a shame I'll have to wait.
Is it chocolate? Is it coffee?
I LOVED the one with lumps of toffee."

But all Grandma heard was a grumbly growl. So she decided to ring back later.

The next day, as soon as
Mum left with Charlie,
the phone rang again.

Brring, brring...
Ted waited for a
few seconds.

Brring, brring...
then he picked it up.

"It's only me," said a cheerful voice.
"Can I borrow Charlie's paints?
I want to make a birthday card."

Ted listened eagerly. Then he
took a deep breath:

"WOW! Brenda, painting's fun,
Especially when the colours run.
Come round tonight and
*   don't forget.*
We'll ALL try out
*   the painting set."*

But all Brenda heard was
a grumbly growl. So she
decided to ring back later.

One morning, Mum put up a new shelf.
Wheeee, whirr, whirr, wheeee! went the
electric drill.

Brring, brring... went the phone. And this
time Ted picked it up straight away.

"It's only me," said a cheerful voice. "Your motorbike has been repaired, and is ready for collection."

"Brrmm! Brrmm!" replied Ted eagerly. Then he took a deep breath:

"I bet it goes just like a rocket,
I'd love to ride in someone's pocket.
I've never tried a motorbike,
But I'm an ace on Charlie's trike."

But all the mechanic heard was a grumbly growl. So he decided to ring back later.

By now Ted was fed up. "I wish I could have a PROPER telephone conversation!" he sighed.

Brring, brring… it was well into the afternoon.

Brring, brring… Charlie wasn't home from school.

Brring, brring… and Mum had gone out in her best skirt.

Brring, brring… "Oh, go away," growled Ted.

Brring, brring… "You won't understand a word I say," he grumbled.

*Brring, brring,
brring, brring…*
on and on the
phone rang.

Until, in the end, Ted snatched it up. And this time
he spoke first:

"*I've had a really rotten day,
THEY'RE ALL OUT, so I can't play.
I need a chat, I'm all alone,
But no one LISTENS on the phone.*"

But someone WAS listening.
In fact, the caller heard every single word!

The caller took a
deep breath and
then he replied:

"I'm Brenda's bear from Number Three,
If you stretch up, then you can see,
I'm waving on the window ledge.
It's brilliant now they've cut the hedge."

"I've got some news, it's really great!
I had to tell, I couldn't wait.
Charlie's been here, did you know?
Sorry, Ted, I've got to go..."

Ted looked across the street in amazement.
He could just see Brenda's bear in the window.
Then Charlie and Mum came hurrying home.

"I can't wait to tell Grandma," cried Mum. And
she dived for the phone. As soon as Grandma
answered, Mum squealed with excitement:

"I got it! I got it! I got the lovely hospital job."

"Oh, NO!" groaned Ted. "Now I'll be
on my own EVEN MORE!"

But Ted was wrong.

Because, when Mum went to work, Brenda's mum became Charlie's childminder. She became Ted's bearcarer too! And Ted began to spend his days with Brenda's bear.

Somehow the two friends never ran out of conversation. And, if ever they missed each other when Ted went home... *brring, brring...*

THERE WAS ALWAYS THE PHONE!

Top Shelf Ted

Melanie's Scruff was a bear with ambition. He liked to explore and make discoveries. And now, more than anything in the world, he wanted to climb up to the Top Shelf.

The Top Shelf was the highest point on the bits and pieces rack belonging to Melanie's mum.

If Melanie's mum left her bedroom door open, Scruff could just see the Top Shelf from Melanie's bed.

One day a parcel appeared on the
Top Shelf, which attracted Scruff like a
magnet. It was an ordinary-shaped box.
There was nothing unusual about its size.
But something about this particular parcel
made Scruff's paws itch.

Before long an afternoon arrived which was ideal for shelf climbing.

Melanie's mum had left her bedroom door open. Recently she had re-arranged the books on the lower shelves.

"A perfect pawhold," smiled Scruff.

And now Melanie and Mum had left for the library.

As soon as he heard
the front door close,
Scruff nipped nimbly
across the landing.

He scrambled
up the first two
shelves with ease.

Shelves three and four were a piece of cake.

Scruff was just planning his attempt on the fifth and final shelf when, "BRRING! BRRING!" The phone rang.

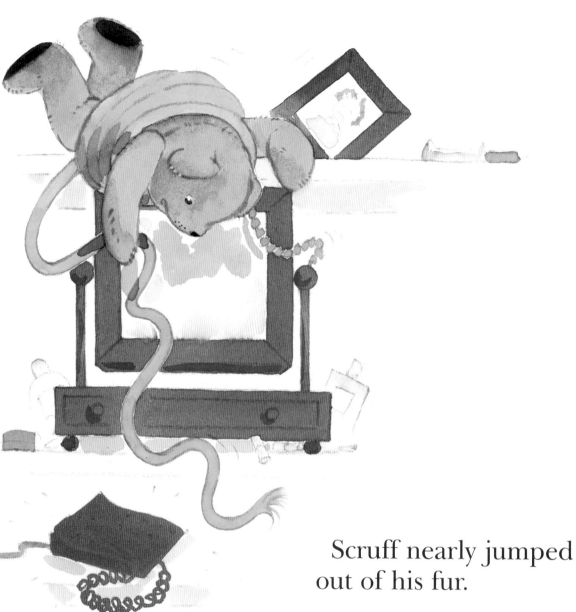

Scruff nearly jumped
out of his fur.

"*Go away!*" he hissed.
"You're making me nervous."

And thankfully, the phone stopped
ringing. Slowly, Scruff began his
countdown.

"*FIVE... FOUR... THREE... TWO...*
WHOOOOSH!"

And with an impressive leap he landed...
on the Top Shelf.

With fumbling paws Scruff attacked the mystery box.

But when, at last, he lifted the lid, he couldn't believe his eyes. Scruff didn't *want* to believe his eyes.

Because inside was a Top Quality, Top Shelf Teddy Bear. Exactly as Scruff had been many hugs and adventures ago.

By the time Melanie and Mum came home, Scruff was flat out on Melanie's bed.

He'd examined his raggedy ear in the mirror…

He'd sighed at the size of the bald patch on his chest…

He'd tried in vain
to wash the paint
from his paws…

But worst of all, he'd
checked out his calendar.

"Just as I thought,"
groaned Scruff.

"It's Melanie's
birthday soon.
*AND THEY'VE
BOUGHT HER A
NEW TEDDY!*"

Later that evening there were
rustling noises across the landing.
Melanie's mum was wrapping the
box from the Top Shelf.

"You *ARE* going to make a little girl
happy," she told the Teddy inside.

Melanie's Scruff covered his ears and tried to sleep.

But pictures from the past kept popping into his head.

Melanie's first day at playgroup…

The terrific train ride they'd taken together…

Trampolining on Melanie's new bed…

The time Melanie had held his paw at the Bear Hospital…

"And now that *NEW* Teddy's going to have all the excitement!" sniffed Scruff.

Next morning Melanie's mum was busy and brisk.

"Visitors!" she explained. "One of my old school friends is coming to see us. And I want everyone," she told Melanie and Scruff, "to be on their best behaviour."

Scruff didn't feel like being on his best behaviour. The last thing Scruff wanted was visitors. So all morning he lay on Melanie's bed and sulked.

But after lunch Melanie
came to fetch him.
She had something
to show him.

"Look, Scruff," cried Melanie. "It's
a brand new baby called Miranda.
And Mum's bought her a brand
new Teddy Bear!

Suddenly Scruff felt like a new bear
himself. Tomorrow he might even go
exploring again.

But just for now, he waited for Melanie to tug at his ear. And whisk him outside for their next adventure!

Are We Nearly There?

Today was the day for Daisy and Dad's journey.

Daisy had been staying with her grandparents.
But now Dad had come to collect her, and to
take her somewhere even more special!

Daisy couldn't wait to set off. So, as soon as they
had said their goodbyes, she began to run —

along the twisty track…

At first Daisy ran as fast as she could. But, little by little, she began to tire.

"Are we nearly there?" asked Daisy. "It's Rabbit," she explained. "He's too *tired* to go any further."

Dad shook his head. But he tucked Rabbit
on top of their rucksack. And Daisy padded off –

along the twisty track …

Daisy and Dad padded side by side.

But suddenly something rumbled.

"Are we nearly there?" shouted Daisy above
the noise. "It's my tummy," she explained.
"It's too *empty* to go any further!"

Dad shook his head. But he rummaged in their rucksack and found the food.

Daisy ate all her own picnic and most of Dad's. For a while she was too *full* to go any further. So Daisy had a little snooze. And before long she felt light enough to dance—

along the twisty track ...

But Daisy wasn't looking where she was dancing.
She didn't see the bed of nettles!

"OW, WOW, WOUCH! Are we nearly there?" wailed Daisy. "It's my paws," she explained. "They're too *hot and stingy* to go any further!"

Dad shook his head. But he blew and he blew until Daisy's paws were cool again and she could bounce –

along the twisty track …

Dad was just getting into *his* bounce when there
was a crackle of lightning.

Next there was a crash of thunder.
And then as soon as the thunder and lightning
had stopped it began to pour with rain.

Daisy didn't like getting wet.

"Are we n-n-nearly th-th-th-there?"
she shivered. "It's my fur," explained Daisy.
"It's too *soggy* to go any further!"

Dad shook his head. But he rummaged in their rucksack and brought out a towel.

"Rub-a-dub-dub. Rub-a-dub-dub," went Dad, until his arms ached and Daisy was warm and dry.

"Ooooh, look!" cried Daisy. "It's a rainbow!"
And she skipped towards it –

along the twisty track ...

The sun grew warm, then hot.

"Phew! Are we nearly there?" panted Daisy.
"It's *meee*," she explained. "I'm too *floppy* to go any further."

Dad flopped down, too. "So am I!" he said.

"Oh, no!" cried Daisy. "Now we'll *never* get there!"

But Dad was already rummaging... right to the bottom of their rucksack.

At last he found what he wanted...

"It's a bottle of Grandma's Famous Fizz," he beamed. "She told me to keep it for emergencies."

Dad held the bottle in a stream to cool it.

"Mmmm!" said Daisy and Dad. And they drank exactly half each.

As soon as they'd finished their fizz, Dad swung Daisy onto his shoulders. Then he carried her –

round the final twist in the track…

And suddenly Daisy could see for herself.
"Look, Dad, look," she cried, "WE'RE NEARLY
THERE! WE'RE NEARLY THERE!"

Dad set Daisy gently on the ground.

"Come *on!*" she told him.

And together they ran the rest of the way—

to the end of the twisty track...

HOME!